Book Eigh

Copyright © 2017

World Teacher Aid All rights reserved.

Contributing Authors

Francis H Clergue Public School- Mlle Phillips

Serenity Bob-Sleeman	Isaac Iyanam
Arley Boudreau	Callie Jansen
Lucas Cruickshank	Gavin Killoran
Mason Dechamplain	Jessie Kirkey
Makenna Duggan-Barnes	Austin Madill
Espen Escasa	Jewels Pyne
Angus Galbraith	Cadence Riseborough
Justice Greeley	Zoe Sheedy
Ellie Harten	Willow Tanninen
Davis Hoffman-St. John	Olivia Whent

Contributing Authors

Francis H Clergue Public School- Jennifer Marengere

Griffin Babineau	Kaitlyn Johnson
Claire Breton	Jordan Lariviere
Sophia Chiarot	Tanner MacIsaac
Luna Chornyj de Dios	Emily Mantha
Amy Clement	Alexis Pellerin
Kate De Beer	Joshua Piche
Dominic Hauser	Lillian Smith
Jorden Haynes	Oliver Smith

Contributing Authors

Francis H Clergue Public School- Mlle. Jessica Barton

Ella Allen	Kassandra Inman
Liam Bumbacco-Franz	Mateo Ivorra
Mariah Case	Pierson Kalomiris
Chase Cerasuolo	Charlee Kennedy
Alyssa Chen	Mackenzie Lambert
Brigitte Guy	Kyle Montgomery
Nathaniel Dewar	Tyson Radford
Evan Dupuis	Avery Shields
Lara Fraser	Benjamin Trevisanut
Isabella Hollingshead	Taber Young

Contributing Authors

Francis H Clergue Public School- Mme Debbie McLean & Peer Leader: Sammi Dechamplain

Jonathan Andrew	Danika Jeffreys
Alexander Beagan	Harley Jolie-Marini
Luciana Herrera	Cecillia Jacques
Joshua Case	Maximus Nielsen
Julian Chenier	Owen O'Leary
Liam Coleman	Luca Paluzzi
Harper Coulter	Alexis Sopha
Harry Fremlin	Jackson Thornton
Rhonda Hermiston	Brianna Wakeley

Contributing Authors

Francis H Clergue Public School- Renee LeClair

Kale Ableson	Graeden Hayward
Ilidio Braganca	Cristiaan Keating
Olivia Briand	Brandon Langlois
Sophie Chilelli	Mason MacWhirter
Bryce Chisholm	Sienna Magli
Helayna Conway	Haylee Palmer
Camden Dubien	Delilah Pearce-Goertzen
Adrianna Fecteau	Kiera Scott
Drew Hankinson	Murphy South
Tiago Harmsen	Zara Zavoral

Contributing Authors

Francis H Clergue Public School- Amy Chojnowski

Kennedy Campbell

Pippa Holmes

Cameron Hurley

Kimora King

Grace McColman

Colton McLean

Malin Moffatt

Serenity Rice

Lorelai Schell

Andrew Shannon

Eva Tuomela

ACKNOWLEDGMENTS

A very special thank you to all those who help make Write to Give happen. Each year, the program continues to grow and have a bigger impact on Canadian and international students. This would not happen, if it were not for the hard work of the teachers who have helped implement this program.

Thank you to our teachers, Mlle. Phillips, Ms. Marengere, Mlle. Barton, Mme. Debbie McLean, Mlle. LeClair, Mlle. Chojnowski & Peer Leader: Sammi Dechamplain.

Thank you to my team of editors, designers and family who have helped with W2G 2017.

Thank you,

Amy McLaren

x

Our New Home

Copyright © 2017

World Teacher Aid All rights reserved.

A sea of red and white flashed before me as everyone stood. The national anthem began to play. "O Canada", I sang, every time I heard the phrase.

As the anthem came to an end, I looked up at my father who had a grin from ear to ear. We followed the crowd who were led by a sweet smell. People were everywhere. There were funny-looking people with bright clothes and big red noses, red and white flags, music playing and sweet smelling food as far as you could see.

We were getting hungry. I showed my Dad where I saw the "flat looking falafels". We were hesitant because we couldn't make out the sign. "P-A-N-C-A-K-E-S- $1.50", it read. "Do you need help?" a kind voice from behind the table spoke. We stepped forward and used our translator to explain our story. It was only our second day in our new country.

The lady explained that today was July first, "Canada Day" she called it. She said that it was Canada's 150th birthday and everyone was gathered around to celebrate this.

Suddenly, loud smashing noises started going off. We looked up to the sky and saw bright lights flickering, they looked like colourful rocket ships. "Fireworks!" everyone in the crowd exclaimed.

I became very scared, so I ran as quickly as I could to get away from the crowds. My father followed as closely as he could. When I finally got somewhere quieter, I looked back hoping to see the bright smile of my father, but he wasn't there.

"Dad, dad, where are you?" I yelled out in my loudest voice.

I began to panic and I could feel blood rushing to my face as my cheeks became warm and red.

My heart was racing in my chest. I saw a washroom symbol and I went inside, hoping it was quiet so I could think of what to do next. I eventually managed to calm down enough to remember I had a picture of my dad in my pocket. I nervously left the restroom with the picture in my hand.

Across the busy crowd I saw a welcoming man wearing a uniform. I recognized the uniform from the airport. When I arrived to my new country, people wearing similar outfits helped my family off the plane. I knew it would be safe to ask him for help. I walked through the crowd and tapped the man on the shoulder. I didn't know how to ask him where my father was, so I pointed to the picture. The man smiled at me and took my hand. I had a good feeling about him.

I followed the man through a big crowd. I was breathing heavily. There were people bumping into me and cheering loudly. My ears were ringing.

All of a sudden, I saw dazzling, red and white lights flashing above me and could hear the beat of a drum that got louder and louder. We got to the front when I realized the lights were coming from a giant platform.

On the platform were many instruments and musicians. There was a big sign that read S-T-A-G-E. As the man led me up the stairs the thudding of the music got louder. When the song was over, the man brought me to the centre of the platform.

My hands were shaking and my belly was rumbling as I looked over the sea of people. The man took my photo, showed the audience, and made an announcement. Out of the corner of my eye, I saw someone running towards me.

Suddenly, I was in the arms of my father and I felt an instant sense of relief.

I was so happy to be with my family in my new country and to be celebrating my first Canada Day with such caring people.

World Teacher Aid

World Teacher Aid is a Canadian charity committed to improving education throughout the developing world with a focus on IDP settlements (Internally Displaced Persons – communities that have been uprooted from their homes). Our current projects are within Kenya and Ghana.

As a charity we are committed to providing access to education for students within settled IDP Camps. We accomplish this vision through the renovation and/or construction of schools.

Before we begin working with a community, we ensure that they are on board with the goal. A community must be settled and show leadership before we commit to a project. We also look for commitment from the Government, ensuring that if we step in and build the school, that they will help support the ongoing expenses, such as teachers salaries, and more.

AUTOGRAPHS

AUTOGRAPHS

Made in the USA
Columbia, SC
07 June 2017